MUCKY
MICKY

ORCHARD BOOKS
Carmelite House, 50 Victoria Embankment, London EC4Y 0DZ
Orchard Books Australia
Level 17/207 Kent Street, Sydney, NSW 2000

First published in 1999 under the title
MICKY THE MUCKIEST BOY by Orchard Books
This updated version published in 2015

ISBN: 978 1 40833 764 6

A CIP catalogue record for this book is available
from the British Library.

1 3 5 7 9 10 8 6 4 2

Printed and bound by CPI Group (UK) Ltd, Croydon, CR0 4YY

MIX
Paper from
responsible sources
FSC® C104740

The paper and board used in this book are made from wood
from responsible sources.

Orchard Books is an imprint of Hachette Children's Group and published by
the Watts Publishing Group Limited, an Hachette UK company.

www.hachette.co.uk

MUCKY MICKY

SPLOT!

Laurence Anholt

Illustrated by Tony Ross

ORCHARD

www.anholt.co.uk

Hee, hee, hello everyone!
My name is **Ruby** and I have the
funniest family in the world.
In these books, I will introduce you
to my **freaky family**.

You will meet people like...

Tiny Tina

Bendy Ben

Poetic Polly

Brainy Boris

Brave Bruno

Hairy Harold

But this book is all about…my
mucky cousin, **MICKY**.

Pooh! What's that **pong**?
It must be Micky. It must be
my cousin, Micky, the yuckiest,
muckiest boy who ever moved.

Micky loves to muck about with a ball. He loves to be in goal.

He loves it most when the field is as wet as a stinky, slimy swamp.

SKID!
SLIDE!
SPLAT!

Now Micky has a filthy face. He has hair like a heap of hay. He has something nasty on his knees.

And poo on his shoe too.

Here is Micky going home.

His dad is waiting on the doorstep.
Micky's dad is not mucky.

Micky's dad is the neatest, tidiest
dad in town.

Micky's dad shouts down the
street,

He makes Micky take off all his clothes...OUTSIDE!

And Micky has to
spend an hour
in the shower.

"There!" says Micky's dad. "Now you are my little angel again."

"Oh pooh!" says Mucky Micky.

One day Micky says, "Look, Dad. Pete is having a party. All my friends will be there."

"Lovely," says Micky's dad. "I will find a special costume for you."

On the morning of Pete's party,
Micky's dad helps Micky put on
the special costume.

A pair of white wire wings.
A twinkly tinsel halo.

And a long angel dress made from a neat white sheet.

"There you are, my little angel," says Micky's dad. "You look sweet in your sheet… PLEASE KEEP IT NEAT!"

Here is Micky going to Pete's party.

Micky meets Mark.

Micky and Mark monkey about in the park.

Micky tries to keep his sheet neat BUT…

"Oh pooh!" says Mucky Micky.
"Never mind," says Mark.
"Have a banana."

Here is Micky going to Pete's party.
Micky meets Megan.

Micky and Megan play alien invaders with Megan's Zappa-Gunge-Gun.

Micky tries to keep his sheet neat BUT…

"Oh pooh!" says Mucky Micky. "Never mind," says Megan. "Have some Space Gunge."

Here is Micky going to Pete's party. Micky meets Max.

Micky and Max make a mucky mud pie.
  Micky tries to keep his sheet neat BUT...

"Oh pooh!" says Mucky Micky. "Never mind," says Max. "Have a piece of pie."

Here is Pete's party.
Everyone is wearing fancy dress.

Here is the fancy dress competition.
The prize is a big box of paints.

But who is this?

"Oh!" says Pete's mum. "It is the most marvellous, magnificent mud monster I have ever seen."

What a surprise. Mucky Micky
wins first prize.

Here is Micky playing with his paints.

Micky tries to keep his sheet neat BUT…

"Oh pooh!" says Mucky Micky.
"Never mind," says Pete. "Have
some jelly and ice cream."

Here is Micky eating jelly and
ice cream.

Micky tries to keep his sheet
neat BUT…

"Oh pooh!" says Mucky Micky.
"Never mind," says Pete. "Have a
big piece of cake to take home."

Here is Micky's neat and tidy dad waiting for his little angel.

Micky's dad sees a small mud
monster coming down the street.
The mud monster is carrying a big
party bag.

"STOP RIGHT THERE!" says
Micky's dad.

Micky's dad makes Micky take
off all his slimy, steamy, stinky
clothes and leave them in a
huge, horrible heap.
Then Micky leaves
squelchy footprints
right up the stairs.
And filthy
fingerprints
on the walls.

Micky mucks about in the big bath like a horrible hog in a bubbly bog…until the bathroom is all brown and beastly, and Micky is squeaky clean.

Here is Micky's dad cleaning
the mucky bath, and wiping the
muddy walls, and washing
the messy clothes...

Until Micky's dad is mucky too.

"Poor old Dad," says Micky.
"I will give him a nice surprise."

Here is Micky creeping into his dad's room. His party bag is full of nice surprises!

Micky hides them...

…then he dives into bed and falls
fast asleep.

"Goodnight, my little angel," says
Micky's dad.

Here is Micky's dad feeling very tired. He climbs into bed. He rolls over. The bed is lumpy. He cannot get comfortable.

Here is Micky's dad finding
Micky's surprises.

A squashy banana,

some green Space Gunge,

a dollop of mud pie,

a beautiful drippy painting
and a nice slice of chocolate cake.

Now Micky's dad is the muckiest man who ever moved.

"OH POOH!" says Micky's dad.

THE END

MY FREAKY FAMILY

COLLECT THEM ALL!

RUDE RUBY	978 1 40833 639 7
MUCKY MICKY	978 1 40833 764 6
POETIC POLLY	978 1 40833 754 7
BRAINY BORIS	978 1 40833 756 1
BRAVE BRUNO	978 1 40833 762 2
TIINY TINA	978 1 40833 760 8
BENDY BEN	978 1 40833 758 5
HAIRY HAROLD	978 1 40833 752 3

Also available
as an ebook